THE GHOST WITCH

Also by
Betty Ren Wright:

A Ghost Comes Calling

The Ghost of Popcorn Hill

THE GHOST WITCH

BETTY REN WRIGHT

Interior illustrations by Ellen Eagle

A
LITTLE APPLE
PAPERBACK

SCHOLASTIC INC.
New York Toronto London Auckland Sydney

ISBN 0-590-48587-3

12 11 10 9 8 7 6 5 4 3 2 1 5 6 7 8 9/9 0/0

Printed in the U.S.A. 40

First Scholastic printing, September 1995

For
Aunt Beth

B.R.W.

To
Zachary, Asher, and Gordon

E.E.

Contents

CHAPTER ONE

The Witch's Cat

"It is too our house now," Jenny Warren insisted. "Miss Nagle left it to us. She and my great-grandma were best friends. My mom helped her out with errands and stuff for years. I guess she wanted to give us a present."

Jenny and her best friend Chris Ellis stared at the big house at the end of Willowby Lane. Dark windows stared back at them.

"That's some present!" Chris rolled her

eyes. "You wouldn't really live here, would you?"

"Maybe yes, maybe no," Jenny said. "We haven't decided yet." She was beginning to be sorry she'd invited Chris to come with her.

"Well, *I* sure wouldn't want to," Chris said. "This is the spookiest-looking house in town. And my cousin says Miss Nagle was a witch!" She looked over her shoulder when she said it.

"That's dumb," Jenny said. "Miss Nagle wasn't a witch. I told you, she was my great-grandma's best friend. Come on," she continued briskly, trying not to notice how dreary the house looked under the gray October sky, "we have to go in and feed Miss Nagle's cat."

"Not me!" Chris squealed. "No way!" She clutched the gatepost as if she thought Jenny might try to drag her up the long walk to the house.

"But that's what we came for!" Jenny exclaimed. "My mom says I have to take a turn once in a while. You don't want the poor cat to go hungry, do you?"

"No, but I want somebody else to feed him," Chris said. "Why don't you take him home with you?"

"Because we can't have a pet in our apartment," Jenny told her. "Later on we might put an ad in the paper to find him a new home. Unless we move in here ourselves. . . ." She tried to sound as if that was what she hoped would happen.

After a moment Chris let go of the gatepost. "You're brave, Jenny," she said. "I wish I was as brave as you."

Jenny was pleased, even if she didn't feel very brave at the moment. "We just have to go into the kitchen," she coaxed. She led the way up the walk and around the side of the house. Leaves crunched noisily under their feet.

Jenny wore the house keys around her wrist on a ring as big as a bracelet. She unlocked the glassed-in back porch with the key her mother had marked for her and scooped up the bag of cat food. Then she opened the kitchen door with a second key.

"Here, Rufus." Her voice seemed to bounce off the walls of the chilly, old-fashioned kitchen.

"What's he look like?" Chris whispered.

Jenny shrugged. "I don't know. My mom's been feeding him till now." She picked up one of the two bowls on the floor in front of the sink. "I'll get the water, and you fill the other bowl with cat food, okay?"

"It's too quiet in here," Chris muttered. Then she screamed. Jenny dropped the water bowl into the sink with a clatter.

"What's wrong?"

"The cat!" Chris whimpered. "He's here, and he's wrapping himself around my legs. Look at him!"

Jenny stared. Miss Nagle's cat was the biggest she'd ever seen. His coat was red-orange, and his green eyes glowed in the dim light.

"The witch's cat!" Chris shivered. She peered into the hallway that led to the rest of the house. "Jenny, let's go," she begged. "I feel as if something's staring at me!"

"That's crazy," Jenny protested. She tried not to notice the prickles on the back of her neck. As she bent to pet the cat, a blast of cold air swept through the kitchen. The door to the hall slammed shut with a crash that made both girls jump.

"Help!" Chris shrieked. She dashed across the kitchen and out onto the porch. Jenny quickly put the water bowl on the floor and raced after her. Hand in hand, they flew down the steps and around the side of the house.

"I t-t-told you that house was haunted," Chris gasped when they reached the gate. "I could tell."

"It's *not* haunted." Jenny tried to keep her voice steady. "The wind blew the door shut, that's all."

"What wind?" Chris demanded. "You

were scared, too, Jenny. You ran as fast as I did."

Jenny knew it was true. "We have to go back and lock the doors," she groaned. "Come on."

Once again Chris grabbed the gatepost. "Not me," she said, and it was clear that this time she wouldn't change her mind. "I'll wait here for you."

With dragging steps, Jenny started back up the walk. She tried not to look at the dark windows or think of the empty rooms behind them. All she had to do was cross the back porch and lock the kitchen door. It was silly to be afraid.

She opened the door to the porch and went through it to the outside of the kitchen. Now just put the key in the lock. She tried to keep her eyes on the keyhole, but she couldn't help one quick peek through the glass pane in the upper half of the door.

The cat was on the counter with his paws tucked under him. *Poor Rufus,*

Jenny thought. *I'm sorry we ran off and left you*. But then she realized the cat hadn't even noticed her. Instead, his green eyes were staring across the kitchen at the door to the hallway.

It was wide open.

CHAPTER TWO

The Dragon in the Mirror

"Of course it was a draft that moved the door," Mrs. Warren said. "What else could it have been, Jenny?"

They had just finished supper and were standing at their living-room window watching old Mr. Barkin pick up soft-drink cans along the curb and drop them into a bag. Mr. Barkin lived in an apartment building a block away. All year long he collected cans to earn money for his Barkin Christmas Fund for Poor Children.

"Old houses are drafty," Mrs. Warren went on. "If we live in Miss Nagle's house, we'll have to get used to that."

"I don't want to live there," Jenny said. "I like it here."

"You *like* sleeping on the couch?" Her mother was amazed. "I thought you hated it. The first thing you said when I told you about Miss Nagle's wonderful gift was 'Now I can have my own bedroom.' "

Jenny thought about the house and those dark, staring windows. She thought about the door that closed and opened by itself.

"I don't mind sleeping on the couch," she said firmly.

"Well, we needn't make up our minds tonight," Mrs. Warren said. "We'll just polish the place up a bit, and then we'll decide whether we want to live in it or sell it. I know Miss Nagle hoped we'd live there. She even left us some money to take care of the taxes every year."

"Who's going to polish it up?" Jenny wanted to know.

"I am. You are. We are—together."

Jenny sighed. Ever since her father died, she and her mother had done lots of things together. Most of the time it was fun, but this was different.

"I'd rather sell it right away," she said.

Her mother just smiled. "No rush," she said. "Maybe you'll change your mind."

Two days later it was Jenny's turn to feed the cat again. "And while you're there, look for my sunglasses, please," Mrs. Warren said. "I'm pretty sure I left them in the dining room yesterday."

"Can't we both go?" Jenny asked. But as soon as the words were out, she was sorry. Mrs. Strauss, their neighbor in the apartment down the hall, had stopped in for coffee, and now she said the same thing she said almost every time she visited the Warrens.

"Too bad you don't have a big strong son to help you, Mrs. Warren. My Bobby is such a help to me."

"Jenny's a good helper, too," Mrs. Warren said. She waggled her fingers at Jenny. "Run along, dear. Don't be late for supper."

Jenny gritted her teeth as she hurried to the back hall where she kept her bike. She knew what Mrs. Strauss would say next. "Jenny is such a skinny little thing. A breath of wind would blow her away. No wonder she has no backbone."

It wasn't fair. *I've got backbone*, Jenny grumbled as she rode across town. *I'm as brave as Bobby Strauss any day*. But when she turned into Willowby Lane, she wasn't so sure. Miss Nagle's house looked drearier than ever.

Rufus meowed a noisy welcome when Jenny unlocked the kitchen door. She shot a quick look through the open door on the other side of the kitchen. Then she filled the food and water bowls, talking to the cat as she worked.

"Good kitty. I wonder if you're lonesome. I wonder if—"

She froze. Was that a noise from the front of the house? It had sounded like a hiss.

Rufus leaped up onto the counter and stared down the hall.

"What is it, kitty? Did you hear something, too?"

Jenny didn't know what to do. She wanted to run—but what if she were running from nothing at all? Then Mrs. Strauss would be right, and Jenny's mother would have to agree with her. *You mean you didn't even pick up my sunglasses, Jenny? I'm surprised at you.*

Stiff-legged, Jenny tiptoed across the kitchen and down the hall. The dining room was on the left, the living room on the right. Both were crowded with heavy furniture. Jenny stepped into the dining room. She saw the sunglasses lying at the far end of the table. Beyond the table was a long, low cupboard with a mirror above it.

For a moment Jenny just stood there. Then she darted the length of the table and snatched up the glasses. As she did, the hissing began again, only this time it was right above her head. She whirled and stared up into the mirror.

A shaggy brown head as big as a laundry basket loomed over her. Cruel eyes glared down, and puffs of steam billowed through gaps in the pointed yellow teeth.

Jenny staggered back against the table, too frightened to cry out. For a moment the head hung above her. Then a great cloud of steam filled the mirror, and when it faded the dragon head was gone. Her own face stared back at her, and behind it the dining room was sunny and still.

CHAPTER THREE

Maybe I Made Him Up

Jenny rode her bike at top speed all the way home. When she got there, Mrs. Strauss and her mother were still sitting at the kitchen table.

"You are so lucky," Mrs. Strauss was saying, when Jenny burst in, "that beautiful big house just waiting for you to move in! A gift from heaven!"

Jenny opened her mouth to tell them about the dragon, but her mother spoke first. "I know we're lucky," she said. She sounded happier than she had in months. "I still can't believe it." She held out a hand to Jenny. "Did you find my sunglasses, dear?"

Jenny looked at her mother's smiling face. Then she looked at Mrs. Strauss. *No backbone*, Mrs. Strauss was probably thinking.

"Here they are," Jenny said. "They were on the dining-room table. I guess I'll watch television for a while." She left the kitchen quickly, before the rest of what she'd wanted to tell her mother could come tumbling out. . . . *A big dragon thing with mean eyes and smoke coming from its mouth!* . . . The words would make her mother's smile disappear. *And I can't even prove I really saw a dragon*, she thought miserably. *If I try to show her, I just know there won't be anything in that mirror.*

The next afternoon Jenny got home from school just as her mother was returning from her job at the supermarket. "I'm going to Miss Nagle's house to do some cleaning," Mrs. Warren said. "You come, too, Jenny. I could use some help."

"NO!" The word popped out so loudly that Mrs. Warren stared at her.

"I mean," Jenny said shakily, "I mean, I don't like it there, Mom. I just don't. It's scary!"

Her mother sighed. "Look, Jenny," she said, "this is silly! You have to give the house a chance. We'll be working together, and it'll be fine. You'll see. The more time you spend there, the better you'll like it."

Jenny shivered. She was sure she would never like it. Never, never, never! But no matter how much she protested, her mother insisted that she go.

Every afternoon that week and the next she and her mother drove across town to Miss Nagle's house. They threw open the windows to let in cool, fresh air while they swept and scrubbed and polished. Each day Rufus waited for them at the back door and followed them from room to room as they worked.

"You see?" Mrs. Warren said at the end of the second week. "Isn't this a great house, Jenny?"

Jenny nodded slowly. Nothing scary had happened to her since the day she'd seen the dragon in the mirror.

"I wonder if I just sort of made him up," she whispered to Rufus one evening. "Like a bad dream." She was sitting in the window seat of the big front bedroom that might be her own room someday. Rufus lay curled up in her lap.

My own bedroom and my own cat, she thought. *Wait till Chris sees this room!*

When she met Chris in the school yard the next morning, her friend had news of her own.

"I just saw Mr. Barkin out looking for cans," she said. "He told me he's going to have a big surprise for us on Halloween night."

"But that's the night of the school party," Jenny objected.

"I know," Chris said. "But Mr. Barkin's surprise is going to happen *after* the party. It's supposed to help raise money for his Christmas Fund."

"What do you think it is?" Jenny wondered. Then she remembered what she'd been waiting to say to Chris. "Want to go to Miss Nagle's house with me after school?" She tried to sound as if the invitation weren't important. "I guess we're going to live there, and I want to show you my bedroom."

Chris twisted her bangs around a finger. "I think I'm busy," she said.

"Please come," Jenny said, forgetting to pretend it didn't matter. "My bedroom is really nice."

"I guess I can go for a couple of minutes," Chris said uneasily. "But I can't stay long, honest!"

That day, school seemed to last forever. Jenny made four mistakes in a spelling test, and she didn't hear her teacher call on her to answer a question. Her fingers kept closing around the ring of keys in her pocket, and each time she touched them, goose bumps peppered her arms. For some reason, the memory of the dragon head returned, scarier than ever.

On the way to Willowby Lane, Jenny decided that she and Chris wouldn't go into the dining room. And they wouldn't look in any mirrors. They would just go upstairs to see the bedroom, and they would feed Rufus, and they would leave.

A nice quiet visit to a nice old house, she told herself. *That's what it will be.*

CHAPTER FOUR

The Terrible Lamp

"It's getting kind of dark, Jenny," Chris said as they rode their bikes into Willowby Lane. "Maybe you should show me your bedroom some other day."

"This'll just take a couple of minutes," Jenny coaxed. "Come on, we'll hurry." If they didn't do it now, she was afraid she'd never get Chris this far again.

They left their bikes at the front gate and made their way up the walk and around the side of the house. Jenny unlocked the door to the back porch and put a finger to her lips. "Listen."

An eager *meow* came from inside the house.

"Rufus is saying hello to us," Jenny said proudly. "We're pals."

She unlocked the kitchen door and bent to pet the big cat. Chris petted him, too, but at the same time she looked around uneasily.

"It's not as cold as it was the last time I was here," she said after a moment. "And it smells different. Nice—like someone lives here."

Jenny sniffed. She smelled cleaning powder and a whiff of the hot chocolate she and her mother had drunk last night. She switched on the overhead light and saw that her mother had left a bouquet of wildflowers in the middle of the kitchen table.

"Come on," she said, "I'll show you my room." She turned on more lights as they hurried down the hall and up the wide front stairs. Rufus tagged behind them, happy to have company.

"Here it is. My room." Jenny stepped to one side so Chris could get a good look at the brass bed and the wide window seat. "My mom says we'll get a new carpet later on."

Chris turned one way, then the other. "It's so big!" she exclaimed. "This is really nice, Jenny. You're lucky!"

For the first time all day, Jenny relaxed. It was going to be all right. Chris wasn't afraid of the house anymore.

"We can go now, if you want to," she offered. "I just have to feed Rufus on the way out." She scooped up the cat in her arms and they went downstairs.

"That's just the dining room in there," Jenny said. "It's nothing special," she added hurriedly as Chris turned to look. "The living room's over here."

Together they peered into the shadowy living room. Jenny reached to turn on a table lamp close to the door and then she hesitated. Perhaps it was because Rufus suddenly leaped out of her arms. Perhaps it was because she was looking closely at the lamp for the first time.

It had a wide tan shade, but it was the base that caught her eye. It was made of thick rings piled one on top of another.

"What's wrong?" Chris demanded. She sounded frightened again.

Jenny could hardly speak. "The—the lamp! The lamp is moving!"

It was true. The rings of the lamp were shifting, swelling, twisting. Jenny knew what they looked like, but she was too terrified to say the word. She felt Chris clutch her arm. Then the rings twisted hard, and the huge flat head of a snake shot out from under the lampshade.

"Jenneeeee!" Chris leaped backward, pulling Jenny with her. Both girls crashed into the doorframe and then into each other. As Jenny struggled to her feet, the snake darted toward her again, its long tongue flicking. The girls raced down the

hall to the kitchen, stumbling over Rufus as they flew out the back door and ran to their bikes.

"We're going over there together," Mrs. Warren said. "Right now."

"No," Jenny said, "I can't."

"Yes, you can," her mother said firmly. "I know something frightened you, but it certainly wasn't a snake wrapped around a lamp. That's just foolish, dear. The living room was probably too dark for you to see anything clearly."

"It wasn't *that* dark," Jenny said. She felt worse every minute as she followed her mother downstairs and out to the car. Neither of them spoke as they drove across town and parked in Willowby Lane.

The back-porch door stood open and both doors were unlocked, just as the girls had left them. Mrs. Warren looked at Jenny sharply, but she didn't scold. Rufus was perched on the counter close to the door. He jumped to the floor and followed Mrs. Warren as she took his dish out to the porch to fill it.

"I'm not going in," Jenny said. She waited on the porch, hardly daring to breathe, while her mother went down the hall to the living room.

After a moment, Mrs. Warren returned. She was carrying the lamp in her arms. "Look at this, Jenny." She set it on the kitchen table and stood back so Jenny could see it from the porch. The overhead light shone on the varnished wood rings that made up the lamp's base.

"I know it isn't beautiful," Mrs. Warren said, "but it isn't a snake either. Just a pile of wood rings, see? I'm sure you must have dusted it when we were cleaning, Jenny. Where in the world did you get that weird idea about the snake?"

"Chris saw it, too," Jenny said. She felt like crying.

"I'm beginning to think Chris is the one whose imagination is working overtime," said Mrs. Warren. "First it's doors that slam shut by themselves. Now it's a snake in the living room." She smiled and gave Jenny a big hug. "Maybe Chris is going to write ghost stories when she grows up."

Jenny wouldn't smile back. Her mother didn't know about the dragon in the dining-room mirror. And she hadn't heard what Chris said when they parted an hour ago.

"Don't ever ask me to go into that house again, Jenny," she'd said in a quivering voice. "Because I'm not going to do it. Even if it means we aren't best friends anymore."

CHAPTER FIVE

Chicken Jenny

The roof of the apartment house was Jenny's favorite thinking-place, especially on cool October evenings. From up there she could see treetops and church steeples all across town. If she looked hard enough, she could even find the tip of Miss Nagle's chimney.

Not that I want to, Jenny thought unhappily. Three days had passed since she and Chris had seen the snake. Before that, she'd been planning where she'd put her things in the big front bedroom, and had wondered whether Rufus would curl up on her bed at night. Now she couldn't bear to think about the house on Willowby Lane.

"Forget about the snake," her mother kept saying. "Your eyes were playing tricks on you, dear. Once we move in, you'll love being there."

But Jenny couldn't forget. With a sigh, she leaned back against the shed that covered the top of the stairwell. She gazed up at the stars. Some nights they twinkled at her in a friendly way, but tonight the huge sweep of sky just made her feel lonely.

Crrrreeak. She sat up straight and looked around. The door on the other side of the shed creaked like that. *No one comes up here, but me,* she reminded herself. *It couldn't have been the door*. She held her breath and waited.

"GOTCHA!"

Jenny screamed as a figure draped in white swooped around the corner and flapped up and down in front of her. For a moment she was too startled to move. Then she saw shiny brown cowboy boots below the white sheet. She had seen those boots before.

She jumped up and gave the sheet a tug. "Get out of here, Bobby!" she shouted. "You are so dumb!"

"Boy, were you scared!" Bobby Strauss pointed his finger at Jenny. "That was really funny!"

"It wasn't funny at all," Jenny stormed. "You'd have been scared, too, if someone sneaked up behind you like that."

But Bobby wasn't listening. "Chicken Jenny," he snickered. "You're even afraid to move into your new house because you think it's haunted."

Jenny stared at him. "Who told you that?" she demanded.

"I heard your mom telling my mom." Bobby pulled the sheet over his head again and danced around the roof in front of her. "Chicken, chicken, chicken!" he howled.

Jenny clenched her fists, but there wasn't a thing she could do except leave. All the way downstairs, she could hear Bobby shouting up on the roof and laughing to himself.

"Everybody else heard him, too," she told Chris at school the next morning. "Now all the people on our block think I'm a scaredy-cat."

"Well, you're not," Chris said firmly. "Anyway, who wouldn't be afraid if they had to live in Miss Nagle's house?"

Jenny groaned. Her friend wasn't making her feel any better.

"I bet it's Miss Nagle's ghost who's haunting her house," Chris went on, peering over her shoulder nervously. "I told my cousin about the snake we saw, and she said that proves Miss Nagle was a witch. Just think, Jenny—the ghost of a witch! That's the worst thing I've ever heard of."

It was the worst thing Jenny had ever heard of, too. She thought about it all the rest of the day. She thought about it so much that she failed her math test.

When she got home that afternoon, her mother was piling empty boxes in the back of the car. "We're going to start cleaning out Miss Nagle's closets," she said. "I'm sure she'd want us to give her dresses and coats to people who need them."

Jenny flinched. "I don't want to go," she said. "Besides, nobody's going to want a witch's clothes."

"A *what*?" Mrs. Warren looked shocked. "What did you say?"

Jenny had never seen her mother so angry. "Chris's cousin says Miss Nagle was a witch," she explained unhappily. "So now she's a ghost witch. And she's haunting that house!"

Her mother didn't answer for a moment or two. Then she bent down to look Jenny straight in the eye.

"Miss Nagle may have been a little odd," she said slowly. "She didn't mix much with other people, but she was a kind and generous person. No one has more reason to know that than we do, Jenny. Besides, there is no such thing as a witch, or the ghost of a witch. Now run upstairs and change into your jeans. I mean it! I'll wait for you in the car."

Jenny ran. Tears filled her eyes, making everything so blurry that when she got upstairs she almost stepped on the long green snake coiled in front of her door.

"Ooohh!" She leaped backward. The snake didn't move, and after a moment she saw why. It was a fake! She looked down the hall just in time to see Bobby Strauss and his friend Jason Foley peek around a corner.

"Gotcha again!" Bobby bellowed. "Chicken Jenny, scared of ghosts and scared of snakes!"

Jenny kicked the plastic snake down the hall. She rushed inside the apartment and slammed the door behind her.

Awful boys! Awful everything! Bobby Strauss was a mean tease. She'd failed her math test. Her mother was disgusted with her. And now she was going to have to get in the car and drive to the last place in the world she wanted to go.

CHAPTER SIX

Rufus Takes Charge

"Just look at this nice big closet," Mrs. Warren said, clearly trying to make Jenny feel better. "Think of all the room you'll have for your clothes and your games."

Jenny stared into the dark closet and thought of just one thing. *A snake could be in there.*

"Put Miss Nagle's clothes on the bed," Jenny's mother went on. "Dresses in one pile, blouses in another, skirts in another. When you get everything sorted, we'll pack some boxes and ask Mr. Barkin where to take them. He knows who needs what in this town." She gave Jenny a hug. "Don't look as if it's the end of the world, hon. I'll be working in the basement. If you want me, just call."

Jenny followed her mother out into the hall. "I'll go down with you and help," she said. "And then we can come back up here and clean out the closet together. Please!"

Mrs. Warren looked grim. "You're not a baby, Jenny," she said. "Everyone has to be alone sometimes, for goodness' sake. Besides," she added encouragingly, "you'll have Rufus to keep you company." She scratched the cat's head and hurried downstairs, humming a little as she went.

As if everything is just great! Jenny thought bitterly. She felt angry for a moment, then ashamed. For months her mother had been sad, missing Jenny's father. Now she was actually singing to herself. That was wonderful—only why did it have to be Miss Nagle's house that made her happy?

The closet smelled musty. Jenny pulled an armful of clothes from their hangers.

"I don't want to clean out this closet," she whispered to Rufus, dropping the clothes on the bed. "I don't want to be here!"

She picked up the cat and sat in the window seat. Outside, the topmost branches of a maple tree moved in the wind. Sitting in the window seat was like sitting in a tree house.

"What am I going to do, Rufus?" she whispered. "I'm so mixed up. . . ."

Rufus snuggled into her arms, and for a minute Jenny felt better. Then the cat sat up. He stared at the door to the hallway, his eyes as big and round as quarters. He'd heard something.

Jenny put him on the floor and stood up.

Now she heard it, too—a scraping noise, as if something very heavy were being dragged along the hallway.

Rufus arched his back. His tail swelled to three times its normal size. He ran to the door, and after a moment, Jenny made herself follow him. Her legs were as stiff as sticks and she could hardly breathe, yet she had to see what was out there.

No! Jenny opened her mouth to scream, but no sound came out. She could only stare at the mammoth crocodile that was dragging itself over the bare floor. Bulging eyes glared at her, and huge jaws stretched into a terrible grin.

"Mom!" It was only a whisper. Jenny couldn't shout; she couldn't move. She could only stand there, terrified, as the crocodile crawled toward her.

Suddenly there was a flash of movement at her feet. Rufus crouched in front of her, hissing and spitting. He looked as small as a kitten as he faced the crocodile.

"Come back," Jenny wailed, but Rufus

didn't listen. When the monster's jaws opened again, he gave a high-pitched howl. Then, to Jenny's horror, he leaped right into the giant mouth.

"Rufus!" Jenny stumbled backward as a puff of smoke filled the hallway. "Rufus, where are you?"

The smoke vanished as quickly as it had come. When it was gone, Jenny saw that the crocodile was gone, too. Rufus stood in the middle of the hallway, licking his fur and looking smug.

"What happened?" Jenny asked. "How did you know what to do?"

Rufus cocked his head. He licked one paw and rubbed it across his ear. Then he padded over to Jenny and looked up at her, green eyes gleaming. *It's okay,* he seemed to say, *you don't have to worry about crocodiles when I'm around.*

CHAPTER SEVEN

The Ghost Witch

"Drat that cat!"

Jenny gave a little shriek and whirled around. Behind her, in the bedroom, stood an old lady dressed in black. She was short and round with rosy cheeks and a fierce scowl. In one hand she clutched a long, pointed stick.

"You keep that animal away from me or I'll turn him into a toad!" she snapped. "He's nothing but a troublemaker!" She waved the stick, and Rufus darted out of sight. Jenny could hear him hissing in the hall.

"Wh-who are you?" she stammered. "How did you get in my bedroom?"

"*Your* bedroom?" The old lady laughed. "This was *my* bedroom long before it was yours, and don't you forget it!"

Jenny clutched the doorknob and wondered if she were dreaming. Little shreds of mist drifted around the old lady, like cobwebs. And her clothes were so strange—a long skirt that swept the floor, a tiny black hat tied in a bow under her chin.

"I-I don't know what you're talking about," Jenny quavered. "This used to be Miss Nagle's house. You're not—"

"I'm certainly not your Miss Nagle!" the old lady exclaimed. "She was a stick—no fun at all, I'm sorry to say. If you must know, I'm her grandmother. Her *famous* grandmother, if you please. In my day everyone in this town knew the witch of Willowby Lane."

"The w-witch?" Jenny felt dizzy. She closed her eyes, then opened them quickly.

"I was a witch, I am a witch, I'll always be a witch," the old lady sang gleefully. "Oh, you were so scared when you saw my crocodile, weren't you? It was lovely! Scared out of your socks—till that pesky cat butted in. I haven't had such a success in years."

Jenny's knees were trembling so much, she could hardly stand, but now she was beginning to be angry as well as frightened.

"It isn't nice to try to scare people," she said. "It's—it's mean!"

"Mean shmean," the old lady chuckled. "Witches are supposed to frighten people. And some folk frighten very nicely—like you, my dear. Some don't frighten at all—my granddaughter, for instance—the one you call Miss Nagle. Oooh, she made me so cross! Wouldn't even look at my wonderful snakes and spiders and dragons and crocodiles. 'Stop that nonsense!' she'd shout when I wanted to do a bit of haunting. 'I've got dusting to do,' she'd say. Oh, she was a bore! And that cat of hers is just as bad. I'm so glad you're coming here to live. I'll try all my tricks and spells on you and your friends. Scary animals are what I'm best at, you know, but I can make all kinds of things appear if I want to. We'll have a splendid time!"

"No, we won't," Jenny wailed. "You can't do that—you can't!" She thought of her mother down in the basement, humming happily as she worked. "I'll tell my mother. She'll make you go away."

The ghost witch smiled slyly. "Your mother doesn't believe in ghosts," she said. "She'll never know I'm in the house. Why, if she were to come up the stairs right now, I'd be gone before she got here. And if you tried to tell her about me, she'd tell you to stop imagining things." She laughed again, a creaky cackle. "It'll be our little secret, my dear. And I'll have a surprise for you and your friends every day. Like this!"

The ghost witch waved her stick, and there was a rush of wings. Rufus screeched from the hallway as a bat as big as an eagle swooped into the bedroom. It dived low over Jenny's head, whizzed twice around the walls, and came to rest hanging upside down from a curtain rod.

"That's just the beginning," the ghost witch said proudly. "Now I'll show you—" She lifted her stick again, but Jenny had had enough.

"No!" she shouted and dashed out of the bedroom and down the stairs with Rufus right in front of her.

The ghost witch's cackle followed her as she ran. "Later, then," she chuckled. "There're lots more surprises where that came from. You'll see, my dear, you'll see."

CHAPTER EIGHT

Mr. Barkin's Surprise

"Why didn't you tell your mom?" Chris wanted to know. She and Jenny were sitting in the farthest corner of the school lunchroom. Their lunch bags were on the table in front of them.

Jenny leaned back and sighed. "But I already did tell her about the snake and about the door opening and closing by itself, and she didn't believe me. What would *your* mom say if you told her there was a crocodile in your upstairs hall and a witch and a bat in your bedroom?"

Chris rolled her eyes. "You're right. My mom would ground me for a month for telling whoppers!" She opened her lunch bag and took out a sandwich. "Did the ghost witch really say she'd make spiders in your house? And dragons?"

Jenny nodded unhappily. She was already sorry she'd told Chris about the ghost witch, but she'd had to tell someone. "That's a secret," she whispered. "Promise."

Chris shivered. "I don't even want to think about it," she said. "Spiders and snakes and dragons make me sick. And a ghost witch makes me sicker than anything."

Jenny reached into her lunch bag for the chocolate cupcake she'd seen her mother wrap that morning. *I'm going to end up being a hermit just like Miss Nagle was,* she thought. *Sooner or later, every-*

one will find out about the ghost witch. I won't have any friends at all. I'll sit in my bedroom window seat all day with Rufus and eat cupcakes all by myself.

When school was over for the day, it seemed to Jenny that Chris was already treating her differently.

"I'm going to find Mr. Barkin and see if he'll tell me what his Halloween surprise is," Chris said. She sounded as if it didn't matter whether Jenny came along or not.

Jenny bit her lip. "Okay, let's," she said. They walked silently down one block and around the corner. Bobby Strauss was playing catch with some other boys in the street ahead of them.

Jenny jumped back. "Let's go through the alley," she said. Chris shrugged and followed.

When they reached Mr. Barkin's apartment building, they went around the side to the shed behind it. He was usually there. Bags of plastic containers lined one

wall, and boxes of cans lined the other. Mr. Barkin was in the middle, tying a bundle of newspaper with cord. He waved when he saw the girls in the doorway.

"Come in, come in!" he shouted. "I'm just decidin' whether I have enough stuff here to borrow my son's truck and run it all out to the recycling center. What can I do for you ladies?"

"Tell us what your Halloween surprise is going to be," Chris said. She giggled and her face grew pink. "We won't tell anyone else, honest!"

Mr. Barkin thought it over. Then he grinned at them.

"All right, I'll do just that," he decided. "You can tell me what you think. The surprise is—I'm going to fix up a haunted house and charge boys and girls to go through it."

He didn't seem to notice Jenny's quick step backward or hear Chris's gasp.

"See, I've still got the old place that belonged to my folks," he went on. "It's too big for one person to live in, but I just can't make myself sell it. What I'll do is buy some of those cardboard skeletons and fix up a few ghosts out of old bed sheets. Then I'll put candles in all the rooms and play spooky music on my tape player. I'm bettin' kids'll pay fifty cents just to prove that they're brave enough to walk through the place. Because it's Halloween and all."

"Not me," Chris said quickly. "I hate haunted houses."

Mr. Barkin looked hurt. "Other towns have haunted houses for Halloween," he said. "They make good money, too."

Jenny tried to cheer him up. "Well, I think it's a great idea," she said. "You can put up signs to announce it."

"That I will." Mr. Barkin's grin came back in a hurry. "It'll be dandy. You'll see."

Later the girls walked to the corner together, once again without speaking.

"I hope it works out," Jenny said finally. "Mr. Barkin will feel bad if it doesn't."

Chris shook her head. "A make-believe

haunted house is different from a real haunted house, I guess," she said. "But I don't like either one." She hurried off, looking unhappy.

All the way home, Jenny thought about Mr. Barkin's surprise. No matter how Chris felt, she knew Mr. Barkin was right. Kids liked being scared, as long as it was Halloween and they knew it was all make-believe. She thought about cardboard skeletons and bed-sheet ghosts. They could be a *little* scary, she supposed, in an old house on a dark night. But would her classmates be really impressed? She hated to think Mr. Barkin might be disappointed.

As she walked, an idea started to grow. It got bigger and bigger, until by the time she'd reached her own apartment building she was running. She raced up the stairs and unlocked the apartment door. The smell of fresh cookies told her what her mother was doing.

She hurried into the kitchen. "Tomorrow after school I'll go to Miss Nagle's house to feed Rufus," she announced. "By myself, okay?"

"You will?" Her mother held out a warm sugar cookie. "That will help a lot," she said. "Good for you, Jenny." She looked as if she couldn't believe her ears.

CHAPTER NINE

The Scariest House Ever

It really is a nice house, Jenny told herself, as she parked her bike at the gate. The wide front porch would look just right with a jack-o-lantern or two. Orange leaves danced across the lawn.

Jenny tried to whistle but she couldn't make a sound. As she walked around the side of the house and unlocked the back doors, her stomach felt as if it were tied in a knot. Even Rufus's warm welcome didn't help much. Coming to Miss Nagle's house alone was hard.

She filled the food dish and the water bowl. "You go ahead and eat," she whispered to the big cat. "And then we'll—we'll sort of walk around together." After that the house was very quiet; the only sound was the *crunch-crunch* of Rufus enjoying his dinner.

Suddenly a terrible squeal ripped the stillness. It sounded like Bobby Strauss hitting a sour note on his trumpet, only a thousand times louder. For a moment Jenny wondered if Bobby were hiding somewhere and playing another trick on her. The squeal sounded again, even louder. With it came thundering footsteps that made the whole house tremble.

Jenny clutched the edge of the kitchen table. A streak of orange flew past her. It was Rufus, heading for the top of the nearest cupboard.

"Come on down, Rufe," Jenny begged. "You were brave before. Please!"

But Rufus just stared at her. These sounds were clearly ones he'd never heard before. The old house echoed with one earsplitting squeal after another, and the footsteps thumped closer.

From where she stood, Jenny could see down the hall. There was one more squeal, and then a huge head loomed from the archway leading into the living room. Ears as big as bed sheets slapped the walls, and a long trunk swept the floor. Tusks gleamed in the dim light of the hall.

An elephant! Jenny choked back a scream. *There's an elephant in Miss Nagle's house!*

Jenny's knees felt like jelly as the elephant moved toward her. He was so big, so LOUD! She could even smell his wild-animal smell. Still clinging to the edge of the table, she took one daring step, then another, toward the hall.

"G-Go away!" she begged. "Go away!"

The elephant reached the kitchen door.

His trunk shot out and wrapped itself around Jenny's waist.

She leaped back, and when she tried to push the trunk away, her hands went right through it.

I can see it, but I can't touch it! she thought dizzily. *It's like fog—AND I'M NOT AFRAID OF FOG.* "Go away!" she shouted hoarsely. "You get out of our house this minute! I'm not afraid of you."

The elephant vanished. But now the doorway was covered with a fine black net—a web! It swayed and trembled as a hairy spider the size of a car tire climbed down from above the doorframe. Jenny jumped backward. She could face an elephant, but the spider was too much!

"I thought that would do it." A cackling laugh came from the other side of the web. Then the spider and the web disappeared, and Jenny faced the ghost witch.

The old lady's eyes were shining. "Now I know what *really* scares you," she chuckled. "Spiders! You should see your face!"

Jenny wanted to run, but she made herself stand still. This was why she had come to Miss Nagle's house alone. She had wanted to see the ghost witch again. She tried not to think about the spider.

"You're—you're really a w-wonderful witch," she stammered. "That's why I came to talk to you."

"Yes, I am," the ghost witch agreed. "Want to see a caterpillar as big as a cow?"

Jenny shook her head fast. "I'd rather tell you about this great idea I have," she said. "It's a way you could scare lots and lots of people—people who *want* to be scared."

The ghost witch scowled. "I don't believe it. No one *wants* to be scared."

"Oh, yes, they do!"

Quickly, Jenny told the ghost witch about her friend Mr. Barkin who was planning a Halloween haunted house. "He's going to feel bad if people don't like his haunted house, but he needs some really exciting ideas," she explained. "If you were there, you could make it the scariest house ever, and lots of people would pay to get in." She looked at the ghost witch's scowling face. "If you were good enough, that is," she added slyly.

"Good enough! GOOD ENOUGH!" The ghost witch's round cheeks turned bright red. "How dare you wonder if I'd be good enough! I could scare this whole town half to death—if I felt like doing it, that is."

"The—the only thing is," Jenny hurried on nervously, "it would be just once a year—on Halloween. And you'd have to promise you wouldn't scare anybody in *this* house ever again. Not ever!"

"Now why would I promise such a thing?" the witch jeered. "Tell me that."

Jenny took a deep breath. "Because if you don't do it, you won't have anybody at all to scare," she said boldly. "When my mom and I move in, I'll get used to your tricks just like Miss Nagle did, and I won't be afraid anymore. And I'll never invite my friends to our house. Not once!"

The witch looked as if she didn't believe a word of it. She waved her stick, and at once the giant spider returned. This time it was on the floor and crawling straight toward Jenny.

Jenny closed her eyes. Then she jumped on the spider and screamed "Get out!" at the top of her voice.

The spider vanished.

"I did it!" Jenny exclaimed. Rufus leaped down from the top of the cupboard and climbed onto her shoulder, purring with pleasure. They both glared at the ghost witch, who looked very cross.

"I can see you're going to be a spoilsport like my granddaughter—your Miss Nagle," the witch said disgustedly. "And just when everything was going so well!"

"What do you think?" Jenny asked eagerly. "Do you like my great idea now?"

The ghost witch paced up and down the hall. She balanced her wand in the middle of the floor and marched three times around it. She sang something to herself that sounded like "Yankee Doodle Dandy" backward.

"Where are all these people who want to be frightened?" she demanded finally. "It's certainly not much fun doing tricks for a naughty girl and a nasty cat who jump on some of my best work!"

CHAPTER TEN

This Is Where I Belong

Jenny told the ghost witch about Mr. Barkin's house. "It's a big old place sort of like this one," she said. "On the other side of town. Mr. Barkin's mother and father lived there a long time ago, but now it's empty. It'll make a great haunted house."

The ghost witch scratched her ear with the tip of her wand. "Maybe it will and maybe it won't," she said sulkily. "You say people will pay money to be scared?"

"Oh, yes," Jenny said. "And Mr. Barkin

will give it all to the poor families in town to buy Christmas presents for their children. You'd be doing a good deed."

"Don't care about that," the ghost witch snapped. "I don't give two hoots and a whistle for good deeds."

Jenny gulped and tried again. "If the haunted house is *very* scary, I'm sure Mr. Barkin will sell tickets again next year. And for every Halloween for years and years and years. You'll be famous!"

The witch's scowl slipped away. "You mean I'd be famous *again*," she said smugly. "I told you before, a hundred years ago everyone in this town knew the witch of Willowby Lane." The scowl came back. "And that's who I am," she said firmly. "I'm the witch of Willowby Lane. This house is my home—always has been. This is where I belong. Why should I—"

She stopped and cocked her head. Then Jenny heard the sound, too—the soft *swish-swish* of footsteps moving through leaves on the walk at the side of the house.

"Wait!" Jenny begged. "Please don't go!" But it was no use. Still scowling, the ghost witch disappeared.

The porch door opened, and then the kitchen door. Jenny's mother came in, her cheeks pink with cold. Rufus leaped down from Jenny's shoulder and rubbed against Mrs. Warren's ankles.

"I was beginning to get worried," she explained, giving Jenny a hug. "It doesn't take very long to feed Rufus. What in the world have you been doing?"

"Nothing." Jenny was close to tears. Her mother couldn't have come at a worse time. *I almost did it,* she thought. *If I just could have talked to the witch for a few minutes more . . .*

But crying wouldn't help. All the way home Jenny went over what she had said to the ghost witch and what the witch had said to her. *She loves scaring people. And she wants to be famous again. Maybe she'll like my idea when she thinks about it,* she comforted herself. But then she remem-

bered the ghost witch's final words: *That's who I am . . . the witch of Willowby Lane. This house is my home. . . . This is where I belong. . . .* She sounded as if she were going to stay right where she was forever.

"Now that you're getting used to the house, I think we should move very soon," Jenny's mother said when they were eating dinner that night. "Oh, Jenny, it's going to be such fun! And just think how pleased Rufus will be to have us with him all the time."

With spiders around every corner and an elephant in the living room! Jenny thought miserably. But she knew it was no use arguing anymore. Not when she'd offered to go to the house all by herself that afternoon. Not when her mother was so happy about moving.

The week dragged by. Jenny and Chris had lunch together in the school cafeteria every day, but they didn't talk about Miss

Nagle's house or about Mr. Barkin's Halloween surprise. Jenny had the feeling that if she even mentioned the ghost witch, Chris would run away from her and never come back.

"What are you going to wear to the Halloween party?" Chris asked Wednesday noon. "My mom's shortening her old prom dress for me."

Jenny shrugged. "I don't know what I'll wear. I haven't thought about it." She'd been too busy worrying about what the ghost witch would do.

"Well, you'd better decide pretty soon," Chris warned. "The party is just three days away, you know."

The next morning Jenny rode her bike to school. As soon as the last bell rang, she raced out of the building without waiting for Chris. With Halloween so close, she had to try to talk to the ghost witch once more. It would be her last chance.

"There goes Chicken Jenny!"

Jenny didn't turn her head to see who

was shouting at her. She knew. *If being scared makes me a chicken, then I guess that's what I am,* she thought, pedaling faster. *But at least I'm trying!* Her heart pounded as she pictured what the ghost witch might do to frighten her this time.

CHAPTER ELEVEN

Jenny Tries Again

The ghost witch did nothing at all.

Jenny let herself in and walked slowly through the house, with Rufus in her arms, switching on lights and peering into each room. She opened and closed closet doors, holding her breath. Every few steps, she whirled around, in case someone or something was creeping up behind her.

"Is anybody here?" Jenny hardly recognized her own quavery voice. "Have—have you decided what you're going to do?"

There was no answer. The house was silent, except for the soft *click-click* of the furnace turning on and off.

When they reached the foot of the stairs, Rufus yawned and jumped to the floor. *He's bored!* Jenny marveled. She wondered how it was possible to be bored, when there might be a monster around any corner. With dragging feet she climbed the stairs alone and tiptoed down the second-floor hall and back.

"I'd j-just like to know—" she began again, but the rest of the sentence trailed off into silence. The ghost witch wasn't going to answer. She didn't want to talk about Jenny's great idea.

Back in the kitchen, Jenny filled Rufus's bowls and stood watching the big cat eat. "It's not fair," she muttered unhappily. "I bet the ghost witch is off planning horrible tricks to play when we move in here. And there's nothing I can do to stop her!"

Rufus meowed and kept on eating.

"I probably made her mad when I tried

to get her to move," Jenny said. "As far as she's concerned, this is *her* house, not ours." She remembered the ghost's final words. . . . *The witch of Willowby Lane . . . that's who I am.*

When Jenny got home, a half hour later, her mother was waiting for her.

"Have you decided what you'll wear to the school Halloween party, Jenny?" she asked. "Time's passing."

Jenny shook her head. "It doesn't matter," she said unhappily. "Blue jeans and an old shirt will be okay."

Her mother smiled and went into the bedroom. When she came back, she was carrying a large box.

"I found this in a trunk in Miss Nagle's basement," she said. "I think it's just your size." She opened the box and took out a long blue skirt and a jacket with puffed sleeves.

"Since we're going to live in a Victorian house, why not dress like a Victorian lady?" she said cheerfully. "This outfit must have belonged to Miss Nagle's grandmother." She held the skirt to Jenny's waist. "It's perfect," she said. "Miss Nagle's grandmother must have been quite little."

She was, Jenny thought. The ghost witch was Miss Nagle's grandmother.

"I don't think—" she began, but her mother wasn't listening. She had lifted a little blue bonnet from the box and now she set it on her own head. "The ribbons tie under the chin like this," she said, looking at herself in the mirror. "You'll have the prettiest costume at the party, Jenny."

Jenny slumped into her mother's rocking chair. She had worried all day about what the ghost witch would decide to do. She had ridden her bicycle across town to Miss Nagle's house and back. She had walked alone through the house, actually begging the ghost to come and talk to her. Now she was just too tired to argue about whether or not she would wear a witch's dress to the Halloween party.

"It's a nice costume, Mom," she said, trying to sound pleased. "I guess I'm pretty lucky."

"You certainly are!" her mother exclaimed. "Who knows what else we'll find in that wonderful old house when we move in!"

That's what I'm afraid of, thought Jenny. But she was thinking of spiders, not dresses. Moving into Miss Nagle's house was sure to bring lots of surprises—all of them bad.

CHAPTER TWELVE

Halloween Night

"I wouldn't want to wear a witch's dress," Chris said, when she and Jenny set out for the Halloween party Saturday evening. "But it's really pretty, Jenny," she added honestly. "I guess it doesn't matter who wore it first. After the party we can go to my house and you can show it to my mom."

Jenny pointed to a poster tacked to a tree. She read it out loud: " 'GOOSE BUMPS! SHAKES! SHIVERS! DON'T

MISS THE HAUNTED HOUSE TONIGHT!' Mr. Barkin's going to be expecting us," she said. "His signs are all over town."

"I'm not going," Chris said. She tripped on the hem of her prom dress and almost fell. "I told you."

"He'll feel bad if we don't come."

Chris pretended not to hear. "Look at the school," she said, pointing down the block. There were lighted jack-o'-lanterns in every window on the first floor. "Come on, Jenny, we don't want to be late."

When they stepped inside the front doors of the school and saw their teacher Miss Cleary at the top of the stairs, both girls laughed out loud. Tonight Miss Cleary was Raggedy Ann. Her bright red hair was braided into thin pigtails to make it look like yarn.

"Right this way, ladies." Miss Cleary pointed down the hall to the auditorium. "My, don't you two look beautiful!"

The auditorium was crowded with boys and girls, parents and teachers. Most of them wore costumes. Game booths dotted the room, and up on the stage a magician was pulling scarves and a pumpkin out of his hat.

"Let's play ringtoss first," Chris said. "I'm good at that sometimes."

Don't think about the ghost witch, Jenny told herself, as she followed Chris across the floor. They both won candy bars playing ringtoss and then moved on to a fishing game. After that they stopped at a booth where you threw balls at a row of black bats with yellow eyes.

"I'd rather duck for apples," Jenny said quickly. She was remembering the huge bat that had swooped over her head in Miss Nagle's house. She hurried to a corner where several boys and girls were bending over big tubs full of water and bright red apples.

When the principal announced it was

time for the grand costume parade, Jenny could hardly believe the party was almost over. All evening she'd been trying not to think about what would or would not happen later at Mr. Barkin's haunted house. Now she was going to find out. Suddenly her hands were clammy. As she and Chris stood in line and walked across the stage so everyone could admire their costumes, she hardly heard the people clapping.

"Let's go to my house," Chris said, as soon as they'd left the auditorium. "My mom will take pictures of our costumes."

Jenny stopped. "I have to go to Mr. Barkin's haunted house first," she said. "Just for a few minutes." *Just long enough to be sure the ghost witch isn't there. She won't be—I know that—but I have to see for myself.*

Chris looked cross. "I told you—" she began.

A crowd of pirates and cowboys burst through the big front doors of the school.

Bobby Strauss, with a black eye-patch and a painted black mustache, led the way.

"Come on, you guys," he shouted, "race you to the haunted house!"

Chris tugged at Jenny's hand. "Let's go home," she said loudly.

Bobby heard her and snickered. "Yeah, you'd better," he scoffed. "Scaredy-cats don't belong in haunted houses."

"I'm not scared," Chris retorted angrily. "Neither is Jenny."

Bobby grinned. "Prove it!" he taunted and raced down the street with his pirate-friends pushing and tumbling around him.

Jenny and Chris watched them go.

"Okay, I'll walk over there with you, Jenny," Chris said finally, "but I won't go inside Mr. Barkin's house. I won't! And I don't see why you want to go there. I think you've seen enough ghosts."

"I have," Jenny said. But she started down the street as she said it.

Other boys and girls came out of the school, and soon a long straggling line of people was headed toward Mr. Barkin's haunted house. Parents were coming, too, on foot or in their cars.

"He wouldn't miss us if we just went home," Chris grumbled. "He'll have lots of customers."

Jenny kept on walking.

When they reached the end of the block and turned the corner, Chris gave a little gasp. Mr. Barkin's house was in the middle of the block, with empty lots on either

side. There were candles flickering in every window, upstairs and down. Gloomy organ music filled the air.

Mr. Barkin, wrapped in a long white sheet, stood at the top of the porch steps. "Right this way, folks," he shouted. "Line up to go through the haunted house. No more than four or five at a time—it's spookier that way."

No one moved. Mr. Barkin reached down to the tape player on the steps and

softened the music. "Come on, boys and girls!" he urged. "Don't be shy. Show us how brave you are!"

"Why doesn't Bobby go first if he's so brave?" Chris snorted.

Jenny looked around anxiously. She wanted lots of people to get in line so Mr. Barkin would earn plenty of money for his Christmas Fund. And she wanted them to be scared by what they saw inside. *Please,* she thought, *let the cardboard skeletons and bed-sheet ghosts be enough!*

Three fifth-grade girls ran up the front walk and dropped their money into the kettle at Mr. Barkin's feet.

"Good for you!" he exclaimed. "Just walk on through, girls. And remember, it's all in fun." He opened the front door and closed it behind them. "Now the rest of you folks line up," he shouted. "The next group can go in as soon as the girls come out."

The crowd giggled and people poked each other, but they didn't get into line.

Jenny realized they were all waiting to see what the first customers would say when they came out.

"I'm going in next," Jenny whispered to Chris. "Somebody has to—"

"EEEEEEEEEEEEEEEEEYYYYYYYY-EEEEEEEE!"

The scream was so loud and so unexpected that Mr. Barkin almost fell off the porch. Another scream followed, and another. Then the door flew open and the three girls came tearing out. Still screaming, they tumbled down the steps and landed in a heap on the walk.

CHAPTER THIRTEEN

The Worst Thing I Ever Saw

For a moment the people standing in front of the house were silent. Then everyone talked at once.

"WHAT HAPPENED?"

"WHY DID YOU SCREAM LIKE THAT?"

"WHAT DID YOU SEE IN THERE?"

The girls giggled and peeked over their shoulders.

"I couldn't help screaming," Sue Bridge said. "It was so real!"

"What was real?" Bobby Strauss wanted to know.

"The worst thing I ever saw in my life," Sue gasped. "A skeleton!"

"I thought that would scare you," Mr. Barkin said. "There's nothing like a skeleton."

"I started upstairs, and he came right down toward me," Sue went on. "I could hear his bones rattling on every step!"

Mr. Barkin looked startled. "Now, wait just a minute—" he began. But then one of the other girls, Terri Euler, broke in. "And there was another skeleton in the living room," she announced excitedly. "He was rocking back and forth in a rocking chair."

"There was one in the kitchen, too," Jean Dennison giggled. "He was stirring something awful in a big black pot."

Mr. Barkin managed to look pleased and very puzzled at the same time. "Now, listen here," he said, but no one heard him except Jenny and Chris. Everyone else was hurrying to get into line, with Bobby Strauss leading the way.

"I'm going in all by myself," Bobby announced. "You can't scare *me* with a lot of make-believe skeletons. I'm not afraid of anything!"

"Good boy!" Mr. Barkin took Bobby's money and gave him a pat on the back.

"What's going on?" Chris muttered. "How could a bunch of cardboard skeletons do all that, Jenny?"

Jenny just shook her head. She watched the front door close behind Bobby and held her breath. "Wait," she said.

They didn't have to wait long. Almost at once, the door flew open and Bobby hurtled out. He leaped off the porch without touching the steps and didn't stop running till he was on the other side of the street.

"What did you see?" Terri Euler shouted. "What are the skeletons doing now?"

Bobby's face was pale in the light of the

streetlamp. "D-Didn't see any s-skeletons," he stammered. "There's a CROCODILE in the front hall. He must be ten feet long!"

"A crocodile?" Someone chuckled, and then the whole crowd started to laugh.

Bobby looked angry. "There is, too!" he insisted. "I saw it."

"Jenny," Chris whispered, "did you hear that? A crocodile! That sounds like the ghost witch. But it couldn't be. . . ." She stared wide-eyed at Jenny. "Could it?"

Jenny nodded happily. The ghost witch was here in Mr. Barkin's haunted house. She had come after all. And she had scared the socks off Bobby Strauss!

"I invited her," she whispered back, "but I didn't think she'd come."

"Maybe I'd better go in and look around," Mr. Barkin muttered. "I'm sure there's nothing there but—"

"Cardboard skeletons and bed-sheet ghosts," Jenny finished the sentence.

"Don't worry, Mr. Barkin. People want to be scared—that's why they came."

Mr. Barkin looked doubtful, but before he could say another word, three pirates and two cowboys dropped their money into the kettle. From then on there was a constant stream of children and grown-ups waiting their turns. One group after another went in slowly and came out fast, to tell what they had seen. There were spiders as big as dishpans in the living room. Giant bats were dive-bombing the kitchen. Headless men were playing checkers at the dining-room table. There were huge snakes, and a gorilla so tall he filled a doorway. There was an elephant!

"I don't know how you do it, Mr. Barkin!" one father exclaimed. "I never saw anything like that dinosaur in the front bedroom."

"Dinosaur!" Chris squeaked. "Did he say dinosaur?"

Mr. Barkin blinked. "Glad you enjoyed it," he said, looking more confused than

ever. "Makin' believe is fun, ain't it?"

"You bet it is," the man said. "Especially when there's someone like you to figure out how to do all this great stuff."

Jenny couldn't stop smiling. "Look at the people," she told Chris. "No one wants to go home. They're all waiting to find out what other people see. And look at all the money in the kettle."

Mr. Barkin heard her and grinned. "Gonna be a great Christmas for lots of kids this year," he said. "There must be something mighty strange in the air tonight. I don't know what folks are seein' but it sure is good for business."

A half hour later when the last customers came running out (they'd discovered a lion crouched in the bathtub), Mr. Barkin announced the haunted house was closed till next year.

"Now all I have to do is blow out the candles and lock up," he said. "You girls want to help me?"

"Not me," Chris said quickly. "I'm not

going in there. I don't care who calls me a scaredy-cat."

"I'll help," Jenny offered. As she climbed the steps to the porch, she looked back over her shoulder and saw Bobby Strauss watching. His mouth opened and closed, but he didn't say a word.

It was just about the best part of the whole evening.

CHAPTER FOURTEEN

A Very Important Difference

Going into Mr. Barkin's haunted house was like stepping into a candlelit cave. One of the homemade "ghosts" was propped in a corner of the entrance hall, and there was a skeleton dangling from a string just inside the living-room doorway.

Mr. Barkin flicked on a light.

"I'll blow out the downstairs candles and check the back door to make sure it's locked," he said. "You can take care of the second floor—if you ain't scared, Jenny."

"I'll be okay," Jenny said. She ran up the stairs before she could lose her nerve.

The upstairs hall was another cave, lit only a little by the candles in the bedrooms on either side. Jenny darted down the hall to the room at the end and then started back, flicking lights on and off, blowing out candles. When she reached the last doorway, she held her breath. If anything were going to happen, it would happen now.

"Don't just stand there," said a voice from inside the room. "Are you coming in or not?"

Jenny peered into the half-dark and then reached around the corner to switch on the overhead light. A small dark figure lay on the bed.

"Nice dress," the ghost witch said sleepily. "But I think it looked better on me than on you. And don't expect me to stir up one more bat or spider or elephant tonight. I couldn't do it if you begged me."

"I won't," Jenny promised. "Did you have a good time?" she added politely.

The ghost witch smiled. She looked cozy and contented, curled up on the old-fashioned bed. "This was the most exciting night I've had in the last hundred years," she said. "I've never heard so much screaming! It was wonderful!" She propped herself up on one elbow and looked at Jenny thoughtfully. "Do you really think all those people will come back next year?"

"Oh, yes!" Jenny exclaimed. "They'll come, and a lot more people besides. Tomorrow morning the whole town will be talking about Mr. Barkin's haunted house."

"And they'll give him all the credit," the ghost witch grumbled. "Well, it doesn't matter, I suppose. You and I know he had nothing to do with it. I was a great witch a hundred years ago—and guess what!"—her eyes sparkled and she pointed her stick at Jenny—"I'm even better now." She leaned back on the pillows. "Run along and let me get some rest. I've certainly earned it."

Jenny didn't move. "There's one more thing," she said. "You *won't* ever haunt Miss Nagle's house again, will you? You promised."

The ghost witch yawned. "Why should I go back there?" she asked lazily. "I'm going to be busy as a buzzard right here, young lady. It's going to take me a whole year to practice some extraspecial, better-than-ever tricks for next Halloween."

"Jenny!" Mr. Barkin called from downstairs. "Are you ready to go home?"

The ghost witch vanished. Jenny crossed the room to blow out the candles in the windows. Then, after a last look at the empty bed, she switched off the overhead light and hurried downstairs.

Mr. Barkin was waiting at the front door. "You look as pleased as a mouse in a cheese factory," he said. "What's up, Jenny? Why the big grin?"

"Well, for one thing," Jenny said, "my mother and I are going to move into a house of our own pretty soon. It's really nice, a lot like this one except—"

There was a squeak from the top of the stairs. Jenny looked up into the shadows and saw a mouse as big as a horse crouched on the top step. It was nibbling a slab of cheese the size of a bucket.

"—except for one very important difference," Jenny said softly. She switched off the hall light and hurried out after Mr. Barkin into the dark Halloween night. "It's not haunted."